# The Stocking Filler

A STORYQUEST BOOK BY
## BECCI MURRAY

For my mum

Writer of the best Christmas poems and
Stocking Filler extraordinaire

# StoryQuest

## CHOOSE THE PAGE - UNLOCK THE ADVENTURE

ISBN: 978-1-9162069-2-2

Published by Llama House Children's Books

\*THE STOCKING FILLER IS AN **INTERMEDIATE LEVEL** STORYQUEST ADVENTURE \*

Welcome to your StoryQuest challenge, the book where YOU are in charge of what happens and YOU are the star of the adventure.

Start your quest on the first page, where your challenge will be explained. At the end of each chapter you'll find two options – choose a page to decide what you want to do next.

As a bonus feature, every StoryQuest book has a SPECIAL CHARACTER hidden amongst the pages. Find the character, and they'll give you a STORYQUEST STAR. This will help you unlock the ultimate ending to your adventure.

There are SO many different paths and SO many different endings – some are good, some are bad, some are happy, some are sad. Which will you choose? Will you complete the challenge? And where will your story end?

Good luck, intrepid StoryQuester, and happy reading!

It's the night before Christmas and all through the house, not a creature is stirring, not even a—

"NAAAAARRRRRRRGH!"

Actually, it sounds like someone *is* stirring.

They're stirring so much they've woken you up.

Rubbing the sleep from your eyes, you climb out of bed and go downstairs to investigate. Dad probably stood on a pine needle. Or maybe Mum's trying to do that new yoga position again, the one where she ties her legs in a knot and sticks her bum in the air.

But it's the middle of the night – your parents are in bed. Dad's snoring like a rhino and Mum's singing Michael Bublé songs in her sleep, so who's downstairs making all that noise?

Curious and a little frightened, you move into the hallway.

"NAAAAARRRRRRRGH!"

There it is again. It's coming from the living-room. You push open the door. The tree lights are twinkling, the stockings are hanging from the fireplace and everything looks just as it should on the night before Christmas. Everything except for that old man doubled over the coffee table. He's ruining the whole Christmassy feel of the place, even if he *is* wearing a

1

red coat and hat, even if his beard *is* as white as snow, even if his tummy *is* wobbling like a bowl full of jelly.

And then you realise – the old man in your living room is jolly old Saint Nick himself!

"*NAAAAARRRRRGH!*"

But he doesn't *sound* very jolly.

As you enter the room, Santa looks up.

"Oh, dear," he grimaces, "have I woken you?"

"It's all right," you reply, "I don't mind. Are you okay?"

"Of course," he says, forcing a painful smile. "I'm always okay. I'm good old Santa, I'm dear old Father Christmas, I'm jolly old Saint *NAAAAARRRRGH!*" He leans on the coffee table again and squashes a mince-pie you left out for his supper. "All right," he sighs, "so I might be having a teensy bit of pain. You see, I had a little mishap. In the chimney. Got bit stuck and hurt my back getting out. It's not the first time and it won't be the last. Either these chimneys are getting smaller or my tummy's getting bigger."

"Can I do anything to help?" you ask.

Santa's eyes twinkle. It's a worrying kind of a twinkle. The sort of twinkle that means something terrifyingly exciting is about to happen.

"Well," he says, "I haven't quite finished my deliveries yet. There are three presents left in the sleigh

2

and three empty stockings to fill. I can't do it myself, not with my back how it is. And my elves are all busy, so…" and he raises a bushy eye-brow.

"You want *me* to deliver the presents?!" you cry.

"Oh, what a wonderful idea! And how kind of you to offer."

"No, I wasn't offering, I just—"

"Here, take the keys to my sleigh and ask the reindeer for directions. You can be my temporary Stocking Filler for the rest of the night."

"But I—"

"When you've delivered all three of the presents, come to the North Pole so you can ring the Magic Yule Bell."

"The magic what?"

"The Magic Yule Bell. Christmas Day doesn't start until somebody rings the bell, and you can't do it until all the presents have been delivered. But here's the thing – a Stocking Filler must never be seen by human eyes. If another human being lays eyes on you delivering those presents, Christmas will be cancelled."

"*Cancelled?!*"

"Don't worry, I have a few things to make your quest a little bit easier," he says, handing you an object.

"It's a phone."

"It is no such thing," replies Santa. "It's a Christmas-Powered Magical Communications Device." (It's a phone.) "If you need my help, just tap on the screen. Oh, you can take this too."

He pulls a bottle from his jacket pocket.

"Fizzy pop," you say, trying to sound impressed and failing.

"I never go out on the night before Christmas without my fizzy pop. It's bad for the teeth but good for the burps – you'll do well to remember that. And last but not least, I've installed an invisibility button inside the sleigh. It only works once a year though, so use it wisely." He pauses and his eyes do that twinkly thing again. "Are you ready for your StoryQuest to begin?"

A surge of excitement runs down your spine.

"I'm ready," you say.

"Excellent. And remember – *don't let anyone see you or Christmas will be cancelled*," and with a twitch of his nose, he vanishes in a cloud of glitter.

Your StoryQuest has begun! Turn to page 38.

As the neighbour's nose presses flat against the window, you push the invisibility button. But the sleigh must've been damaged in the crash, and instead of vanishing the button sets off an alarm.

A shrill noise blares out of the sleigh.

*BLEEEEEEP! BLEEEEEEP! BLEEEEEEP!*

The woman with the massive nose flings open her window, and shouts, *"SOMEONE'S STOLEN SANTA'S SLEIGH! YOU'LL BE ON THE NAUGHTY LIST FOR THIS, YOU THEIVING YOUNG RASCAL!"* and you don't wait around to find out what the rest of the village say.

You've been seen by Manesh's nosey neighbour. Go back to the start of the book or turn to page 18 to make a different choice.

A swig of Santa's fizzy pop is just what you need. *GLUG, GLUG, GLUG, GLUG…*

Ahhh, that's better!

With your newly-found energy, you lower yourself into the red chimney. It's full of spider-webs. You're fairly sure one of the critters has gone up your trouser leg.

When you reach the fireplace, you see a young girl asleep in her bed. She must be Ellie. You take out the present, feeling thrilled to be making your first delivery, and place it quietly and carefully into the—

*BAAAAAAAAAAAAAAARP!*

The burp blasts out of you like a ship coming into a port, shaking the room like an earthquake.

Ellie sits bolt upright in bed. She stares at you for a long moment. And then, "You're not Santa!" she cries, close to tears. "*MUUUUUUUUM!*"

You've been seen by Ellie, but…

Wait, there must've been magic in that burp of yours, for as soon as it leaves your mouth *time goes backwards*.

You and the present are transported back up the chimney and into the sleigh, and in seconds you're flying through the air again towards Ellie's house. The fizzy pop has magical powers and it has given you a second chance to deliver the present without being seen – marvellous!

To go back in time, turn to page 45.

You take out your Christmas-Powered Magical Communication Device (it's a phone) and call Santa. He appears on the screen wearing a very smart dinner jacket.

"Do you like my outfit?" he asks. "My back's feeling much better now, so I thought I'd get ready for the party. How are the deliveries going?"

You tell him Dasher is sulking about not having a carrot.

"Well, he *is* fond of a carrot or two," replies Santa. "That's why I keep a few spares in the sleigh."

You check under the seat. There's a brown bag with a dozen fresh carrots inside – hurray! You hold one out to Dasher and he seems to perk up, snatching the vegetable out of your hand and chomping it down in one bite.

*CHOMP!*

"Thanks, Santa," you say.

You have two parcels left to deliver. Where do you want to go next?

To deliver Amy's present, turn to page 66.

To take Manesh's gift, turn to page 61.

You dart out from the tree like a ninja and run towards the window – you can hide behind a curtain.

But a bauble falls off one of the branches. It's a sturdy little devil and it doesn't smash when you stand on it, but it sends you flying into the air, where you turn a somersault before landing on Justin's feet.

His eyes are glazed, like he hasn't slept in six months.

"Do you know where the nappies are?" he asks, not caring who you are or why you're in his living-room.

You've been seen by Manesh's dad, but you've learnt that a little *rest* does a *lot of good*.

Go back to the start of the book and use what you've learnt to complete the challenge.

You take flight and head for the hill, where you land in the keep of a Medieval castle. You're not sure why you think Amy lives in a castle, but, still, it's a nice view from up here.

A troupe of ghostly soldiers carrying long swords and heavy shields burst out of the wall with their weapons raised.

"Ye shalt not trespass in ye olde castle," cries one of them, "lest the wrath of King Bourbon de Biscuit shalt smite ye down like a doggeth!"

You have no idea what he just said.

But it didn't sound very welcoming.

"I don't want to cause any trouble," you tell him. "I'm just trying to deliver this present."

"Well, bless my battle axe," says the ghost, eyeing the gift, "it hast been six centuries since anyone gaveth *me* a present. Hand it over, ye young intruder, and we shalt speaketh no more of this in the morrow."

He takes Amy's present and opens it up to find a pretty white nighty inside.

"Great bludgeons and clubs," he smiles, "this is just what I needeth."

And he certainly looks more ghost-like when he puts it on.

You've lost your final present. But you were *so close* to completing the challenge. Don't give up now!

Go back to the start of the book or turn to page 76 to make a different choice.

You make a run for the stocking and hope for the best.

*CREEEEEEEAK!*

*CREEEEEEEAK!*

*CREEEEEEEAK!*

*CREEEEEEEAK*

You're fast, so the noise doesn't last long and then you're there at the end of the bed. But just as you reach for the stocking, *just* when you think you've delivered your first present, Ellie stirs in her sleep.

"Santa," she murmurs, "is that you?"

Your heart leaps to your throat. If she sits up, you'll be seen and Christmas will be cancelled.

There's only one thing for it – you'll have to hide!

To hide in the wardrobe, turn to page 65.
To duck behind the bed, turn to page 40.

Calling a reindeer is more difficult than you think. When you whistle, there's only *one* reindeer who's listening – and that's Dasher. He's really enjoying those funny sounds you're making. In fact, he thinks it's a song. He's stamping his feet in time with your whistling, crashing and thumping and hammering the roof with his big heavy hooves until he wakes up the dogs in the neighbouring building.

*YAP! YAP!*

*WOOF! WOOF!*

*BARK! BARK!*

A light comes on from inside the pound. The front door opens and a man appears. He points a torch in your face.

You've been seen by the dog warden. Go back to the start of the book or turn to page 60 to make a different choice.

13

You decide to call Santa.

Taking out your Christmas Powered Magical Communications Device (it's a phone), you press the CALL SANTA button.

A jolly face with a white beard pops up on the screen. It's Santa. He's back in the North Pole, and he's swapped his usual red outfit for a pair of stripy pyjamas and a fluffy pink dressing-gown. He's drinking something that looks like gone-off custard from a tall glass.

"Hello," he says, swigging his eggnog. "How are the deliveries going?"

"Only one left," you tell him, "but I'm at Amy's house and I can't get in. Look," and you hold the phone up so Santa can see the problem.

"Ho, ho, ho!" he chortles. "I'm afraid the reindeer have played a little joke on you. They always do that with the last delivery. Amy doesn't live *in* the lighthouse – she lives *next to* the lighthouse. Can you see that little house over there?"

You look. And there, like a tiny doll's house on the edge of a cliff, is a small building.

"I see it," you reply.

"Excellent," says Santa. "Once you've made the

delivery, come straight back here and join us at the Christmas party. I can't wait to eat all of those yummy mince-pies – even grown-ups deserve a treat at Christmas, you know," and with that final piece of advice, he hangs up the phone.

The reindeer fly you up to the roof of Amy's house. You climb down the chimney to find the embers in the fireplace are still warm. There's an elderly lady asleep on a rickety bed in the corner. She has an artificial tree with old-fashioned decorations and a bowl on the table with a single satsuma in it – there's no stocking.

Have you gone to the right place?

No, leave the cottage and turn to page 76.
Yes, put the gift on the old lady's bed and turn to page 56.

You use your Christmas-Powered Magical Communications Device (it's a phone) to call Santa. When you press the button, his face pops up on the screen. He's getting ready for the Christmas party and he's wearing his best paper-hat.

"Ah, my temporary Stocking Filler," he says. "How's everything going?"

"Not too well," you admit. "Dasher's being a bit of a handful."

"Dearie me," says the man, "that reindeer is a little terror when he meets someone new. An elf had better finish the deliveries. I'll get one sent out to you right away. Thanks for your help."

Santa hangs up the phone. An elf materialises next to you and you're transported back to your house in a cloud of glitter. Remember what you've learnt about that naughty reindeer and try the challenge again.

StoryQuest over. Go back to the start of the book.

You'd like to ask a reindeer to fly you onto Manesh's house.

The thatched roof will just about hold your weight, but only if you're careful. Two reindeer have volunteered for the job.

Who would you like to choose?

To choose Prancer, turn to page 49.

To choose Dasher, turn to page 63.

You swerve left and narrowly miss the tree. But the reindeer keep running and you hurtle across the grass, heading straight for Manesh's garden. The white picket fence splinters like matchsticks as you plough through it.

*SMAAAAAAAAAAAASH!*

That was loud.

Hurriedly, you check the surrounding windows to see if anyone has heard the commotion. A light comes on in an upstairs room. Someone shouts, "What's all that racket?!" and you almost jump out of your skin.

Oh no, you've woken one of the neighbours!

The curtains twitch and a long nose pokes out from between them. It presses against the glass as if made out of putty. It belongs to the nosiest neighbour in the whole village – you'll need to think fast or she'll see you.

To press the invisibility button, turn to page 5.
To pretend the reindeer are a Christmas decoration and hide, turn to page 77.

You go down the grey chimney, squirming through the hole like a giant worm until you reach the empty fireplace below and you find yourself in a dark basement.

It's creepy down here. The only light comes from an old-fashioned skylight in the corner; a grubby window leading up to the pavement outside. It allows the orange streetlight to trickle in through a metal grate and lights the bare walls with an eerie glow.

Strangely, there are no Christmas decorations and no stockings. In fact it looks more like a storage room than a house. There's a stack of cardboard boxes piled against the opposite wall, each of them labelled CHUMMY PAL DOG FOOD, and a steep flight of concrete steps leading up to a wooden hatch in the ceiling.

It must be a doorway into the house. Perhaps Ellie's stocking is upstairs. What do you want to do?

To go up the steps and look for the stocking, turn to page 79.

To phone Santa, turn to page 39.
19

You choose Dasher to lead the way.

He's *very* excited. It's like he's never been chosen for anything before in his life, because…well, he's never been chosen for anything before in his life.

Dasher quickly loses interest in the moth and instead starts prancing around like a kangaroo with its tail on fire, leaping from foot to foot and shaking his antlers with joy. His bouncing jolts the sleigh. Two of the presents slide under your feet.

One is labelled For Ellie.

The other is To Manesh.

Whose parcel would you like to deliver first?

If you'd like to deliver Manesh's gift, turn to page 85.

To deliver Ellie's first, turn to page 70.

You unscrew the cap of the fizzy pop bottle and take a swig. It's gingerbread flavour with a hint of stuffing (Santa's favourite). The bubbles collect in your stomach, and suddenly—

*BAAAAAAAAAAAAAAAARP!*

Wow, that was gassy!

The burp makes you feel better, plus, it must've had magical powers. Because suddenly *time goes backwards.*

The presents reappear in the sleigh, the invisibility button is un-pressed, and everything goes back to how it was before you hit the tree.

You've been given a second chance to deliver Manesh's present – awesome!

To go back in time, turn to page 61.

You steer the sleigh into Manesh's front garden to avoid the milk-float. There's a inflatable Santa decoration on the driveway and it gives you an idea.

Quickly, you hide under the seat of the sleigh.

"Keep still," you hiss at the reindeer. "Don't move a muscle."

The float stops in front of the house. A milkman gets out. He takes two bottles of semi-skimmed from the back and then walks into the garden. He looks at the giant Santa, then back to the nine life-size reindeer.

"Nice Santa," he mutters. "Shame about the reindeer. Not very realistic. These Christmas decorations get worse every year," and with that, he puts the milk on Manesh's doorstep, goes back to his float and drives away.

You breathe a sigh of relief as you crawl from your hiding-place and looking up at the roof you realise it's a thatched cottage. The delicate structure won't hold the weight of nine reindeer and a sleigh, so you'll have to find another way to reach the chimney.

To climb up the drainpipe, turn to page 67.

To ask a reindeer to fly you there, turn to page 17.

The red chimney is full of spider-webs. You're fairly sure one of the critters has gone up the leg of your trousers. It's a long, slow climb (the chimney, not your trouser leg) and by the time you reach the fireplace, you're tired, achy and covered from head to toe in soot.

Nervously, you duck through the fireplace and into the room.

As your eyes adjust to the darkness, you find yourself in a child's bedroom. There's a girl asleep in her bed. She must be Ellie. A stocking hangs from the end of it, just the right size for her present.

You move towards it.

*Creep, creep, creep…*

*Tip-toe, tip-toe, tip-toe…*

*CREEEEEEEAK!*

Uh oh, the floorboards are old and squeaky! They're going to wake up the girl and your adventure will be over before it has hardly begun.

What are you going to do?

To keep tip-toeing, turn to page 54.

To make a run for it and hope for the best, turn to page 12.

You cross your fingers – what else is there left to do? You've delivered all three of the presents now, so perhaps it doesn't matter if you're seen.

Then again, perhaps it does.

The plane pulls up next to the sleigh and the passengers are looking out of the windows. You've been seen by —

Wait. Who *have* you been seen by? Remember, Christmas will only be cancelled if you're seen by another human being.

But the whole plane is chock-a-block with magical characters, some you recognise, some you don't, and all smiling widely as they pass. They must be going to Santa's party too! There are elves and pixies, gingerbread people, the Easter Bunny, two small dragons, a coven of good witches, Jack Frost, the tooth fairy and various talking woodland animals wearing clothes.

Santa said you mustn't be seen by another human being – and you haven't been!

With a sigh of relief, you follow the plane across the frozen landscape to an enormous ice palace. There's a banner above the entrance saying 'WELCOME TO SANTA'S PARTY', and a moat around the outside full of melted chocolate. The walls glisten as if carved out of jewels, the roof shines gold like sunlight and a troop of guards are spinning giant candy-canes in honour of your visit.

And there, in front of the palace, surrounded by a multitude of cheering elves, is Santa himself.

"Welcome," he says, as you land the sleigh. "What a wonderful Stocking Filler you are! You took a few wrong turns along the way, but you kept going and that's what matters. You should be very proud of yourself. Now, before you ring the Magic Yule Bell and start Christmas, do you have the StoryQuest Star for me?"

If you collected the StoryQuest Star from Fairy Berry, turn to the page you saw glittering on the object when she handed it over.

If you didn't collect the StoryQuest Star, you're still awesome. Turn to page 74.

25

You decide to break one of the lighthouse windows. It's a terrible idea, not to mention illegal. At the sound of smashing glass, the lighthouse keeper comes running downstairs.

"I've called the police!" he yells. He's not been this angry since someone stole his light-bulb. "They'll be here any minute so you'd better explain yourself, you little vandal!"

You've been seen by the lighthouse keeper. Try again to see if you can complete the challenge.

Go back to the start of the book or turn to page 80 to make a different choice.

*Chomp!*

You take a quiet bite of the carrot. Mmm, it's delicious – just what you need after delivering your first present.

But there's a rumbling noise coming out of the fireplace. It sounds like someone is falling down the chimney, and then – *CRASH!* – Dasher's head bursts out of the grate and snatches the carrot.

*CHOMP! CHOMP! CHOMP! CHOMP!*

The bedroom light is switched on.

That wretched reindeer has woken Ellie.

*"MUUUUUUUUM!"* she shouts. "THERE'S A REINDEER IN THE FIREPLACE!"

You've been seen by Ellie. But you've delivered one present, so well done, mighty Stocking Filler!

StoryQuest over. Go back to the start of the book and use what you've learnt to complete the challenge.

"Ho, ho, ho!" you chortle, doing your best Santa impression from down on the floor. But here's the thing – Santa is an old man with a deep voice and you're…well, you're *not* an old man with a deep voice.

Ellie throws back her covers and peers over the end of the bed.

"*MUUUUUUUM!*" she yells, at the top of her lungs. She's so loud, there are fish at the bottom of the North Atlantic Ocean who hear her. "THERES AN ELF IN MY BEDROOM AND YOU SHOULD SEE THE SIZE OF ITS EARS!"

Rude.

You've been seen by Ellie. Go back to the start of the book or turn to page 54 to make a different choice.

You choose Comet to lead the way. She's a bit drowsy, but at least she's not chasing moths.

Above you, the stars twinkle and a crescent moon lights the sky. Everything is so still, so peaceful, so Christmassy – there's adventure in the air!

In the back of the sleigh there are three presents. You can see the labels of two. One says, To Amy, and the other is, For Ellie.

Whose present would you like to deliver first?

To go to Ellie's house, turn to page 45.
If you'd rather take Amy's gift first, turn to page 66.

You throw the nappies onto the sofa.

What a great shot you are! They bounce off one of the cushions and tumble onto the middle seat, where they sit quietly as if having been there the whole time.

Manesh's dad turns. He sees the nappies on the sofa, the one he has just been searching, and scratches his head.

"That's weird," he mutters. "I'm sure they weren't there just a—"

"JUSTIN!" cries Manesh's mum. "WE HAVE A CODE BROWN *AND* A CODE YELLOW! GET A MOVE ON, JUSTIN, HURRY UP!"

"Coming," he sighs tiredly.

Then he picks up the nappies and heads out of the living-room.

Quickly, you clamber out through the branches. You run to the fireplace, put Manesh's present into his stocking and dive into the grate, where you make the long journey back up the chimney as fast as your legs can climb.

You've done it – you've delivered Manesh's present! Awesome!

Exhausted, you collapse onto the thatched roof. The reindeer and sleigh are hovering level with the chimney, but you're not sure you have enough energy for the next delivery right now.

What do you want to do?

If you want to carry on and deliver the last present, turn to page 42.

If you want to go somewhere quiet for a rest, turn to page 36.

To land the sleigh and calm Dasher down, you search for an open space. You see a large garden with a tall fence. The lawn is flat and soft – it looks like the perfect place to land.

With a pull of the reins, the sleigh flies lower. But Dasher pulls at his harness and the carriage thumps heavily onto the lawn before skidding into a rose bed.

It's the biggest display of flowers you've ever seen (or at least it *was* until you flattened it). You don't see flower beds like this in just any old garden, and that's because this isn't just any old garden – it's *the Queen's garden.* You've landed in the grounds of Buckingham Palace!

As Dasher chomps down the remains of Her Majesty's roses, you see four guards patrolling the side of the palace. Their tall busby hats make them look like enormous bears in the moonlight.

You should fly away before one of them sees you.

Okay, but I'd like to swap Dasher for Comet first.
Turn to page 45.
Let's go now and leave Dasher in charge. Turn to
page 59.

"Wooooo-ooooooo! Wooooo-oooooo!"

It's your most terrifying voice. You're really going for it, giving it everything you've got, and as ghost impressions go it's up there with the best.

Most young children would definitely run away screaming.

But Ellie is not like most children. Ellie plays scary video games and likes a good jump-scare. Ellie reads books about ninjas and watches murder mystery films. And now, in one slick movement, Ellie flings open the wardrobe door and grabs you by the scruff of the neck, tossing you over her shoulder and pinning your face to the carpet.

From this angle, you can see the karate certificates on her bedroom wall.

"*MUUUUUUUUUM!*" shouts the girl, and your Christmas adventure comes to a painful end. But you leave a little wiser than you began.

Go back to the start of the book or turn to page 65 to make a different choice.

You take out the Christmas-Powered Magical Communications Device (it's a phone) and call Santa. His face pops up on the screen. He's wearing a woolly jumper with bright flashing lights and someone has painted his face to look like a reindeer.

"I've delivered all three of the presents," you tell him, "but I need you to ring the Magic Yule Bell for me."

"No problem at all," smiles Santa. He picks up a big, brass bell with a silver handle. It sparkles as if lit by a thousand tiny fire-flies. "I'll ring it right now so Christmas Day can begin. Oh, and I can't thank you enough for all your hard work – you are a truly fantastic Stocking Filler. Merry Christmas!"

## *DING DING DING DING DING DING DING!*

Suddenly, the world around you seems brighter. A warm feeling grows in your chest. And as the sleigh dissolves into a cloud of glitter, you find back in your own bed.

It's Christmas morning. There's a stocking on the floor. In it, there's a gift. You take it out and read the label.

To my super Stocking Filler,
A little thank you for all your hard work.
From Santa

Excitedly, you tear open the paper. It's a book, all about a young human being who saved Christmas by becoming the best Stocking Filler the world has ever not-seen.

And the star of that book…is you.

Congratulations on completing the challenge – you're a marvellous human being!

If you want to find the Ultimate StoryQuest Ending, go back to the start of the book and try again.

You leave Manesh's house to go somewhere quiet for a rest. There's a small park nearby. No-one's around at this time of night, so you land the sleigh to take a breather.

Suddenly, one of the bushes starts to move. There's someone coming out of it and there's no time to hide.

But as the leaves part you see a small lady in a silver tutu. There's a holly wreath on her head and her skin glows like sunlight in the darkness.

"Blimey, en't you an 'ard one to catch up with," she puffs. "I've been followin' you since that Ellie girl's house. Oo, my poor achin' bones."

The woman turns to take something out of the bush. She has a pair of glittery wings on her back.

"Are you a fairy?" you ask.

"That's right," she replies. "Fairy Berry's the name. I'm Santa's chief baker."

"Wow, that sounds like a fun job."

"Does it?" snorts Fairy Berry. "Well it en't. That jolly old so-and-so don't understand the logistics of baking six billion cakes in one go. *Your cakes are divine,* he says. *I'll hand them out on Christmas night,* he says. *Just one for every person on the planet,* he says. What is it you people think? – that a fairy can wave 'er magic wand and yummy treats just pop out of 'er oven?"

That's *exactly* what you thought, but you don't say so.

"What sort of cakes do you make?" you ask her.

"Duh!" she replies. "Fairy cakes, obvs. Anyway, I en't got time to stand around chattin'. Flour to sieve, eggs to crack. I'm only 'ere to give you *this*."

She holds out a star. The moonlight catches it and the number 47 glistens on one side.

"A StoryQuest Star!" you cry, taking the gift.

"When you've finished making your deliveries, take it to the North Pole for the ultimate end to your challenge. Anyway, gotta go. Sugar to sprinkle, icing to spread. Ta-ta!" and she slips away into the darkness as fast as she arrived.

Congratulations – you've found the StoryQuest Star!
Memorise its number then turn to page 42.

When the glitter clears you find yourself on the roof of your house. There's a magnificent sleigh in front of you. It has golden seats and a silver carriage, with tiny diamond-like stars embedded into the runners. You climb into the driver's seat and take hold of the reins.

At the front of the sleigh, nine reindeer are harnessed together in pairs. Each has a collar with a silver nametag. The two at the front are called Comet and Dasher, but only one can guide your way.

You study the reindeer carefully. Comet breathes a cloudy yawn into the chilly night air and blinks her eyelids with a heavy sigh. Dasher on the other hand is more awake, but a little distracted by a moth. Choose your reindeer carefully and your journey will begin.

If you'd like to choose Dasher, turn to page 20.
If you'd prefer Comet to lead the way, turn to page 29.

You phone Santa and explain the problem.

"Oh dearie, dearie me," he says, "it sounds like you're in quite a pickle. This quest is going to be harder than I thought. I'll send a replacement at once – you can come to the North Pole and help with my party instead," and before you know it, an elf appears at your side.

She sprinkles a handful of magic dust onto your head and you're immediately transported into Santa's ice palace, where he puts you in charge of the washing-up.

Try the challenge again once you've finished the dishes.

StoryQuest over. Go back to the start of the book to try again.

You duck behind the bed just as Ellie sits up. She doesn't see you, but she turns on the light with a soft *CLICK!* before putting both feet on the floor.

Uh oh, she's getting out of bed.

She starts to walk. One step, two steps, three steps, four, towards an open doorway and out onto the landing, where she disappears into the opposite room and closes the door behind her.

Phew, she's gone to the bathroom. You've never been so excited to see someone go into a bathroom in your whole entire life!

With lightning speed, you spring up from the floor, shove the girl's present into her stocking and run towards the fireplace.

*CREEEEEEEAK!*

*CREEEEEEEAK!*

*CREEEEEEEAK!*

*CREEEEEEEAK!*

*CREEEEEEEAK*

*CREEEEEEEAK*

The noise doesn't matter.

You'll be back in the chimney and gone by the time she comes back.

But when you reach the fireplace, you see a carrot

on the floor near the grate. Ellie must have left it there for the reindeer. Do you want to pick it up?

To pick up the carrot and risk getting caught, turn to page 58.

Forget the carrot – I'm getting the heck out of here! Turn to page 73.

You're feeling tired as you start your journey to the final house, but Amy lives on an island and the crisp sea-air keeps you awake. The water flashes silver in the moonlight as you skim the calm surface with the runners of your sleigh. There are no fishing boats out at this time of night and no sound can be heard except for the gentle lapping of the waves.

In the distance, you see a light. It's too bright for a streetlamp, and as you grow nearer you realise it's coming from a lighthouse.

This could mean trouble. Any lighthouse keeper worth his salt will notice nine reindeer and a sleigh flying towards him. How are you going to get past without being seen?

To call Santa and ask his advice, turn to page 39.
To press the invisibility button, turn to page 80.

Heading back to the cellar, you creep towards the hatch. You reach down and take hold of the handle, but it won't open – the hatch must have locked when you closed it.

One of the dogs picks up your scent. It walks to the front of its cage and sniffs the air.

*YAP! YAP!*

"Shush," you hiss. It will alert the warden of the pound if you're not careful. "Good doggy, go back to sleep."

*YAP! YAP!*

Its barking wakes a second dog.

*WOOF! WOOF!*

*YAP! YAP!*

"No, please stop," you whisper. "You won't get any leftover turkey if Christmas is cancelled."

More dogs wake up. They're excited by the sight of a new visitor, wagging their tails and joining the chorus.

*BARK! BARK!*

*WOOF! WOOF!*

*YAP! YAP!*

Suddenly, a man appears at the end of the corridor. He shines a torch in your face. You've been seen by the warden at the dog pound. Christmas is cancelled, but at least you've made some new doggy friends.

Go back to the start of the book to try again, or turn to page 79 to make a different choice.

With a gentle pull of the reins you find yourself moving through the night sky towards Ellie's house with Comet leading the way. The streetlights grow small beneath you and the buildings look like miniature doll houses – it really is a magnificent view.

You travel fast, and it's not long before the reindeer swoop past a tall tower block, down a road with trees growing out of the pavement, through the spokes of an enormous Ferris-wheel and along a row of semi-detached houses, where you land on one of the roofs with a bump.

There are two chimneys: one made of red bricks, one made of grey. They're side by side – there's no telling which chimney belongs to Ellie's house and which belongs to next-door.

You'll have to go down one and take a look.

I'd like to go down the red chimney. Turn to page 23.

I'd rather take the grey one. Turn to page 19.

You're sick over the side of the sleigh and it goes all over the two remaining presents – you can't deliver them in *that* state.

Sad times.

Oh well, you've learnt to be careful around the invisibility button. Use this information wisely and you'll do better next time.

Go back to the start of the book or turn to page 82 to make a different choice.

You take the StoryQuest Star out of your pocket and hand it to Santa.

"You found it!" he smiles. "That's wonderful news! And because you collected the StoryQuest Star, you get to make a Christmas wish." He hands you a big brass bell with a silver handle. It sparkles as if lit by a thousand tiny fireflies. "Just ring the Magic Yule Bell and wish away."

This is it. Your challenge is complete. You're going to start Christmas *and* make a wish.

You take a breath, close your eyes and…
*DING DING DING DING DING DING!*

A shower of soft snow bursts from the sky and a pile of beautifully wrapped presents appears on the ground. Through the windows of the ice castle, you see tables spring up from the floor all covered in delicious treats and snacks, including an enormous chocolate fountain big enough to take a bath in and a huge carrot for the reindeer.

A fir tree grows out of the ice. Its branches are covered with flickering lights, shiny tinsel and sparkling baubles, and the whole group of magical characters gather around it to sing about a young human being who saved Christmas by becoming the best Stocking Filler the world has ever not-seen.

And then…*your Christmas wish comes true*.

For there in the sky, nine reindeer are flying towards you. They're pulling a golden sleigh, and this time it's carrying the most important gift of all – your family and friends.

"An excellent wish," nods Santa. "Christmas is always the most special when you share it with those you love. Merry Christmas, everyone!"

Congratulations – you've found the Ultimate Ending to your story and won yourself the best Christmas *ever!*

You choose Prancer to fly you up to Manesh's chimney, so you remove his harness and climb onto his back. He carries you carefully up the thatched roof before placing you down on the straw.

That was great reindeer-choosing – you can always rely on Prancer.

You walk to the chimney and lower yourself in. There's a bird's nest near the entrance, but you climb around it and before long find yourself in the fireplace of a dark living-room.

There's a green sofa, two flowery armchairs and a baby-bouncer. Four stockings are hanging from the mantlepiece. There's a Christmas tree in the corner, a real one, with twinkling lights and Christingle oranges. The smells drift up your nostrils and fill you with memories of the Christmas season: the scent of pine needles, the orangey zest of the decorations, the faint whiff of…the faint whiff of…

Hm, what *is* that other smell?

"JUSTIN!" A woman's voice comes out of the adjoining room. What are the residents of Manesh's house still doing up at this hour? "JUSTIN, I NEED YOU TO BRING ME SOME NAPPIES! CODE BROWN, JUSTIN, CODE BROWN!"

So *that's* what the smell is.

A man's voice replies from upstairs.

"Keep it down, Gita. You'll wake Manesh."

"THE NAPPIES ARE IN THE LIVING-ROOM!" she replies, ignoring his request. "SERIOUSLY, JUSTIN, HURRY!"

You hear the man's lazy footsteps trundling down the staircase.

*Step, step, step, step, step…*

He'll be here any second.

Thinking fast, you dash behind the Christmas tree. The pine needles prickle your skin, but it's a great place to hide. You can wait here until they've changed the baby's nappy, then put the present in Manesh's stocking and leave.

The boy's father enters the living-room. He's still half-asleep. He's searching for the nappies, but he can't find them, rummaging amongst the cushions of the sofa, looking on both of the arm-chairs and scrabbling under the rug, all without success.

He's still looking when you notice a packet on the floor near your feet. Oh crikey – *the nappies are right here next to you!*

"I can't find them, Gita," calls Manesh's dad, turning his back to your hiding-place. "Are you sure they're in the living-room?"

"YES!" comes the urgent reply. "THEY'RE IN THE CORNER, BEHIND THE TREE! HURRY, JUSTIN, HURRY!"

Uh oh.

To change hiding places while Justin's not looking, turn to page 9.

To throw the nappies onto the sofa behind his back, turn to page 30.

You fly to the bottom of the hill, land on the roof of the bungalow and go down the chimney.

There are no decorations, no tree, no presents. The wallpaper is grey, the furniture is grey, the ceiling is grey and the carpet is…well, it's beige, but it's not the happiest carpet you've ever seen.

There's a sign on the wall saying, 'Santa Don't Stop Here', and another that reads, 'Christmas is Pants.'

Suddenly, a large net drops from the ceiling. It lands on your head, smelling old and musty. Your arms and legs become tangled – you can't get it off!

It's a trap.

A very stinky trap.

A trap for…

"Got you this year, Santa!" cries a grumpy-faced man, bursting into the room. He's wearing a t-shirt with a picture of a dead Christmas tree on it and a grey Santa-hat. "You can stay here in my miserable house until all the ho-ho-horrible jolliness has gone out of your rosy red cheeks and your belly doesn't wobble like a bowl full of—" He stops and peers into the net. You're not what he was expecting. "Who the heck are *you?*"

The grumpy-faced man kicks you out his house.

52

You've been seen and your adventure is over, but well done for delivering two of Santa's presents. Keep going – you've almost completed the challenge!

Go back to the start of the book or turn to page 76 to make a different choice.

You tiptoe over the squeaky floorboards.

*CREAK...*

*CREAK...*

*CREAK...*

You're doing well, you're almost there. But you're so busy concentrating on being quiet you don't notice a toy car at the end of the bed. Your foot hits it and you slip. Not just a little slip but a great big one. The sort of slip where your feet go over your head and you land in a heap like a crumpled ball of paper.

Ellie wakes up with a start. She can't see you down there on the floor, but she knows something or someone has woken her up.

"Santa?" she says, sleepily, "is that you?"

To say nothing and hope she goes back to sleep, turn to page 83.

To say, "Ho, ho, ho!", turn to page 28.

You decide to accept your fate and do nothing.

Ellie opens the wardrobe door. She stares right at you. At least, you *think* she's staring at you, but her eyes are closed. And then you realise – she must be sleep-walking! It's lucky you didn't so something silly to wake her up, like pretending to be a ghost.

"Stop putting baked-beans on the cat," she murmurs. "It's not winter and it smells like turquoise. Just get the kettle on, Nigel, or I'll karate-chop your salad."

You're not sure what to say to that.

But you know you should say *something.*

"Erm, listen," you reply, "I'll put the baked-beans away and all that, but only if you go back to bed," and miracle of miracles, that's exactly what she does.

As her head hits the pillow, you breathe a sigh of relief and sneak back to the fireplace. Ellie has left a carrot for the reindeer by the grate. You love carrots. Do you want to eat it?

Yes, please. To take a bite, turn to page 27.
You're not hanging around for a carrot. To grab it for the deer and get the heck out of there, turn to page 58.

You decide this must be the right house and place the present on the old lady's bed. After all, even grown-ups deserve a treat at Christmas.

Suddenly, everything around you glitters as if made of gold and a warm feeling fills the room. You've done it! You've delivered all three of the presents without being seen! You're the best Stocking Filler *ever!* All you need to do now is go to the North Pole and ring the bell to start Christmas.

Back into the chimney, out onto the roof and up into the dark sky you go.

The reindeer travel north, away from the lighthouse, away from London and away from the green countryside, until the air becomes frostier and great ice-bergs litter the sea below. They leap through the clouds, excited to be heading home for Christmas, but there's a low rumbling noise pushing in from the south.

It sounds like an engine.

A big jet engine.

And it's getting closer by the second.

Looking over your shoulder, you see the plane. It's coming your way and fast. It'll be side-by-side with the sleigh in no time and all the passengers will see you.

You can't give up now, not on the last leg of your quest!

What are you going to do?

To press the invisibility button, turn to page 62.
If you'd rather act casual and hope for the best, turn to page 87.

You grab the carrot and climb into the chimney. The cobwebs cover your face and a spider runs out of your trouser-leg, but still you scramble to the top of the chimney where the reindeer are eagerly awaiting their treat.

You've delivered your first present! Brilliant!

Feeling proud, you gaze up into the velvety night sky. It's a little cloudy now. Wisps of grey slide across the moon and the air feels damp. You'd better get a move on before the rain starts.

Taking the two remaining presents from the back of the sleigh, you see one is addressed To Amy, the other is For Manesh.

Where to next, intrepid Stocking Filler?

To deliver Amy's present, to page 66.
To go to Manesh's house, turn to page 61.

You leave Dasher in charge and head for the skies.

But the excitable reindeer won't fly. Instead, he runs out of the palace garden and slams into an enormous statue of Queen Victoria with his great antlers. Her Majesty cracks in two, each half of her crashing down to the ground in a noisy explosion of dust.

The Queen's Guard hear the commotion, despite the big furry hats covering their ears, and run to confront the intruder.

You've been seen, but remember what you've learnt so far to try again or make a different choice.

Go back to the start of the book or turn to page 32 to make a different choice.

You sneak past the sleeping dogs, all the way along the corridor to the front door.

Quietly and slowly you turn the latch…

*CLICK.*

You push open the door, closing it gently behind you and…

*CLICK.*

You've made it safely out of the dog pound without being seen. Phew!

From the pavement outside, you look up at Ellie's house. The reindeer are waiting for you to come back, but how will you get onto the roof?

There's a plant climbing the wall between the two buildings. Its stems are thick and it looks sturdy enough to hold your weight. Either that, or you could ask one of the reindeer to come down and fly you back up.

What would you like to do?

If you want to try climbing the plant, turn to page 71.

To call a reindeer, turn to page 13.

Manesh lives in a small village to the north of London. It's a long way, but the reindeer move swiftly and soon they're leaving a trail of magic-dung all over the countryside. A herd of cows have settled down for the night on the grass. The poo falls onto their heads, sending the poor creatures floating up into the air like giant balloons.

It's lucky there's no-one around to hear their mooing, or you might've been spotted.

Waving goodbye to the cows, you soar over a dense woodland, past a lake and along a small country lane. Orange streetlights are flickering in the distance and a church steeple marks the centre of a nearby town.

Manesh's house is next to the village green. There's a circle of terraced houses with thatched roofs, tiny windows and narrow chimneys. You're so busy admiring the loveliness of his home that you don't notice an old oak tree in the middle of the grass.

Quick, do something – you're going to crash!

To swerve right, turn to page 90.

To swerve left, turn to page 18.

You press the invisibility button, but nothing happens.

What was it Santa told you at the start of your quest?

*"I've installed an invisibility button inside the sleigh, but it only works once a year."*

Oh no, you've already pressed the button once and the plane's getting closer. The passengers will see you and all your hard work will have been for nothing.

Time to panic!

Call Santa and ask him to ring the Magic Yule Bell for you. Turn to page 34.

Cross your fingers – what else is there left to do? Turn to page 24.

Dasher is so excited he slips his harness and runs to the sleigh. He sticks his snout under your legs, flicks you up into the air and catches you on his back, where you cling to his ears like handle-bars as he takes to the sky.

Soon you've landed on the thatched roof of Manesh's cottage. Dasher carefully places you down, but he has a funny look in his eyes. It's the sort of look that says, "Mmmm, yummy, that looks like a tasty snack," and before you can stop him the naughty reindeer has taken a huge bite out of the thatched roof...

*CHOMP!*

And the whole lot comes thundering down into Manesh's bedroom.

*CRASH!*

You land on the bed in a mountain of straw. You've *definitely* been seen this time. Drat that pesky reindeer!

☆

Go back to the start of the book or turn to page 17 to make a different choice.

You scoot up the tree like a rocket-fuelled squirrel, right to the topmost branch where you hide amongst the twigs. The whirring of the electric milk-float grows nearer. It stops near the village green and out climbs the milkman. He takes two bottles of semi-skimmed from the back of the van, sees the reindeer, not to mention the enormous golden sleigh with the diamond-encrusted runners, and frowns.

Confused, he puts down the milk and comes over to investigate. Dasher is so excited to see him he puts both hooves on his shoulders and licks his face. The milkman laughs then takes out his phone.

"Yes, police please," he says. "There's a sleigh on the village green, reindeer and all. I'll stay with them until you get here."

The reindeer are taken to a nice little animal park in the forest and the sleigh is towed away. The milkman even takes the presents to a local charity shop. You won't be able to complete the challenge now – try again soon.

Go back to the start of the book or turn to page 84 to make a different choice.

Ellie's wardrobe is next to the fireplace, so you nip inside and close the door.

You hear Ellie get out of bed – uh oh. Then the floorboards creak as she moves towards your hiding place – double uh oh. She's getting nearer and nearer, closer and closer, until she suddenly takes hold of the handle and pulls at the door.

Perhaps the wardrobe isn't such a great hiding place after all.

How will you get out of *this* one?

Make a noise like a ghost to scare her away. Turn to page 33.

To accept your fate and do nothing, turn to page 55.

You set off towards Amy's house and find yourself flying over a beautiful moon-lit ocean.

A lighthouse sits on a distant clifftop with a tiny building perched next to it. In the early night, the fishermen are out on their boats – you'll need to stay quiet to avoid being spotted.

Of course, this would be easier if Dasher wasn't bouncing around like a rubber ball and snorting so loudly. You'll be seen if he doesn't stop it.

You'll have to take action and fast!

If you'd like to phone Santa and ask his advice, turn to page 16.

To fly the sleigh into the clouds, turn to page 89.

The drainpipe going up the side of Manesh's house is cold, slippery and difficult to climb. You place your feet against the brickwork and walk up the wall like an insect, but as you near the top you hear a horrible creaky sort of a noise – *the pipe is coming away from the wall!*

You climb faster, scrambling up the drainpipe as it slowly moves from the house, and somehow you manage to reach an upstairs window-ledge with your foot. You stand on it to haul yourself up to the thatched roof, treading carefully so you don't fall through its delicate structure.

Crikey, that was some climb!

You walk to the chimney and lower yourself in. There's a bird's nest near the entrance, but you climb around it and before long find yourself in the fireplace of a dark living-room.

There's a green sofa, two flowery armchairs and a baby-bouncer. Four stockings are hanging from the mantlepiece. There's a Christmas tree in the corner, a real one, with twinkling lights and Christingle oranges. The smells drift up your nostrils and fill you with memories of the Christmas season: the scent of pine needles, the orangey zest of the decorations, the faint whiff of…the faint whiff of…

Hm, what *is* that other smell?

"JUSTIN!" A woman's voice comes out of the adjoining room. What are the residents of Manesh's house still doing up at this hour? "JUSTIN, I NEED YOU TO BRING ME SOME NAPPIES! CODE BROWN, JUSTIN, CODE BROWN!"

So *that's* what the smell is.

A man's voice replies from upstairs.

"Keep it down, Gita. You'll wake Manesh."

"THE NAPPIES ARE IN THE LIVING-ROOM!" she replies, ignoring his request. "SERIOUSLY, JUSTIN, HURRY!"

You hear the man's lazy footsteps trundling down the staircase.

*Step, step, step, step, step…*

He'll be here any second.

Thinking fast, you dash behind the Christmas tree. The pine needles prickle your skin, but it's a great place to hide. You can wait here until they've changed the baby's nappy, then put the present in Manesh's stocking and leave.

The boy's father enters the living-room. He's still half-asleep. He's searching for the nappies, but he can't find them, rummaging amongst the cushions of the sofa, looking on both of the arm-chairs and scrabbling under the rug, all without success.

He's still looking when you notice floor near your feet. Oh crikey – *the nap next to you!*

"I can't find them, Gita," calls Manesh's dad, turning his back to your hiding-place. "Are you sure they're in the living-room?"

"YES!" comes the urgent reply. "THEY'RE IN THE CORNER, BEHIND THE TREE! HURRY, JUSTIN, HURRY!"

Uh oh.

To change hiding places, turn to page 9.

To throw the nappies onto the sofa, turn to page 30.

As Dasher leads the sleigh towards Ellie's house, you find yourself soaring over London with the wind in your hair. The buildings and vehicles look like toy cars and doll's houses from up here, and the river looks more like a stream.

But suddenly, Dasher's zipping around all over the place. He's so excited he can't fly in the right direction, and he's threading the sleigh in and out of lampposts, spinning around church spires and loop-the-looping over Big Ben.

It'll be *next* Christmas by the time the presents are delivered at this rate.

What do you want to do?

If you want to land the sleigh and calm Dasher down, turn to page 32.

To call Santa, turn to page 16.

The plant looks sturdy enough to climb, so you take hold of the stems and – *OUCH!* – realise you're climbing a rose bush.

It's difficult to avoid the thorns, especially with nine reindeer staring down at you like you're the latest instalment of their favourite television programme, but you finally get there and pull yourself up to the roof.

Your hands are sore. Comet rubs her face affectionately against your arm then licks your wounds. It feels gross, but there must be magic in that slimy reindeer spit because your cuts and scrapes immediately vanish.

Amazing!

All this climbing is thirsty work though. Do you want to take a swig of fizzy pop before going down the red chimney?

No, thank you. Turn to page 23.
Yes, please. Turn to page 6.

To cheer up the sulky reindeer, you decide to tickle his tummy. All animals like having their tummies tickled, right? Apart from tigers and lions and panthers and…well, *reindeer*, as it turns out.

You see, reindeer are very sensitive about their tummies. The slightest touch sends them running away from the tickler as fast as their hooves will carry them. And *this* reindeer isn't called Dasher for nothing.

Like lightning he darts from the roof, taking the other poor harnessed reindeer with him and sending Santa's sleigh crashing down into Ellie's garden.

*KABOOM!*

Every light in every window in every house on the street lights up. The neighbours are fascinated by the sight and they're also wondering why there's a child on the roof of number 14.

You've been seen by every person in Ellie's neighbourhood, but well done for delivering one present. Keep trying – the more you learn, the sooner you'll complete Santa's challenge.

Go back to the start of the book or turn to page 73 to make a different choice.

You decide there's no time for the carrot – you've got presents to deliver!

But when you climb back up the chimney, you find Dasher leaping from hoof to hoof like a rabbit on a pogo-stick. He can smell the carrot and was expecting you to bring it for him. After all, that's what Santa usually does.

When he sees your empty hands, he sits down and folds his hooves in a sulk. You won't be flying anywhere until you make him feel better.

The question is, *how?*

To tickle his tummy, turn to page 72.

To call Santa, turn to page 8.

"That's okay," replies Santa. "You don't need the StoryQuest Star to ring the Magic Yule Bell." He hands you a large brass bell with a silver handle. It sparkles as if lit by a thousand tiny fire-flies. "Go on, give it a shake."

You take a deep breath, excitement fluttering your tummy, and ring the bell.

*DING DING DING DING DING DING DING!*

A shower of soft snow bursts from the sky and pile of beautifully wrapped presents appears on the ground. Through the windows of the ice castle, you see long tables spring up from the floor, all covered in delicious treats and snacks, including an enormous chocolate fountain big enough to take a bath in and a huge carrot for the reindeer.

A tall fir tree grows out of the ice. Its branches are covered with flickering lights, shiny tinsel and sparkling baubles, and the whole group of magical characters gather around it to sing a song about a young human being who saved Christmas by becoming the best Stocking Filler the world had ever not-seen.

"What a wonderful temporary Stocking Filler you are," smiles Santa. "This is going to be a very merry

Christmas indeed. And it's all thanks...to *you*."

Congratulations – you've completed the StoryQuest
challenge! You're awesome!
Go to the start of the book if you want to find the
Ultimate Ending.

This must be the wrong place, so you leave the tiny house and scan the coastline for other buildings.

There's not much around, but you can see a hill with a castle on the top of it and a bungalow at the bottom. You get a lot of castles and bungalows near the sea – nobody really knows why and you don't have time to care.

Which building do you think Amy might live in?

To check out the castle, turn to page 10.
Let's try the bungalow. Turn to page 52.

You pretend to be a Christmas decoration by shouting, "Freeze!" at the reindeer and hiding under the seat of the sleigh.

It's a *great* plan! Every garden surrounding the village green has some kind of Christmas decoration in it: a glow-in-the-dark snowman, a light-up holly tree, mechanical penguins, flashing fairy lights, solar-powered elves with moving arms, and a singing candy-cane that spins around to the tune of Auld Lang Syne. There's even an inflatable Santa right there next to you.

But none are quite so impressive as the ornamental sleigh in the garden of number 14 (the one with the life-size reindeer and the diamond-encrusted runners).

Carefully, you watch the woman next door through the wooden slats of the bench.

Her nose swells against the glass. Two beady eyes pop out from above it. They ogle the magnificent sleigh with a jealous squint. The only decoration in *her* garden is a small Santa-hat she placed on the head of a gnome, and she's so wrought with jealousy, she sticks her nose in the air and closes the curtains with a huff.

Phew, that was a close one, but you'd better leave the sleigh where it is in case she looks out of the window again.

How will you get onto the roof without it?

I'll climb up that rusty drainpipe. Turn to page 67.
I'll ask a reindeer to fly me there. Turn to page 17.

You go up the steps to search for the stocking.

The wooden hatch creaks as you open it. It's not much lighter upstairs than it is in the cellar, but you can just about make out a long hallway *full of cages* and in each cage is a dog.

This isn't a house – it's the local dog pound!

There are all kinds of dogs in here: big ones, small ones, fluffy ones and ones that are completely bald except for a small tuft of hair on their heads, and luckily they're all asleep.

This is definitely *not* Ellie's house.

What do you want to do?

I'll sneak past the dogs and leave through the front door. Turn to page 60.

I'd rather go back into the cellar and up the chimney.

Turn to page 43.

You press the invisibility button and one by one the reindeer vanish. Then the sleigh vanishes too. And when you look down you can't see your legs and you're soaring across the sky with nothing holding you up except the soft ocean breeze.

It's awesome, and so much better than any rollercoaster you've ever been on.

As you approach the cliff-face, you pull on the reins and feel yourself moving gradually lower and lower, until fifty-four invisible hooves touch the ground and your carriage bumps to a halt.

Excellent invisible-sleigh driving skills!

The lighthouse keeper can't see you from here, so you press the invisibility button once more and everything returns to normal.

But Comet is nodding her antlers towards the lighthouse.

"What is it?" you ask. "Do you want me to go in there? You mean, Amy lives in a *lighthouse?* Cool."

Excitedly, you pick up the present. You've never been in a lighthouse before and this is your last stop before you go to the North Pole to ring the Magic Yule Bell. Yippee!

But the lighthouse has no chimney. In fact, it

barely has a roof, just a big glass dome on the top of it. How will you get inside?

If you want to break a window, turn to page 26.
To call Santa, turn to page 14.

Bravely, you prepare to jump out of the sleigh.

It's a long way down, but the grass should cushion your fall. You lift one of your legs over the side and balance on the edge of the carriage, but as you raise your second leg you accidentally hit the invisibility button with your foot.

The whole sleigh, including yourself and the nine reindeer, vanish into thin air and the suddenness of it turns your stomach. You're floating above the treetops with nothing holding you up and it's making you feel a bit sick.

In fact, it's making you feel *really* sick.

You can't hold it in much longer.

What are you going to do?

To have a swig of fizzy pop, turn to page 21.

To be sick over the side of the invisible sleigh, turn to page 46.

When you don't reply, the girl called Ellie settles down on her pillow and falls back to sleep, and you breathe a sigh of relief.

Phew!

A little bruised, you get up off the floor. You place the present into Ellie's stocking, being careful to avoid that pesky toy car, then quietly tiptoe back over the squeaky floorboards towards the fireplace.

You notice a carrot lying next to the grate. Ellie must've left it there for the reindeer, but you've always liked carrots. Plus, they help you to see in the dark, which might be useful when you're delivering the next two presents.

Do you want to eat the carrot or take it back up the chimney for the reindeer?

I'm not hanging around any longer. To grab the carrot and get the heck out of there, turn to page 58.

A carrot? – heck, yes! To take a bite, turn to page 27.

Landing the sleigh on the village green is going to be tricky, but you're willing to give it a go.

With your heart in your mouth, you lean to the left and steer the sleigh under that pesky branch. Then you lean to the right and it swerves to the other side of the tree, where the reindeer pace the air as if treading water in a swimming pool, until, "Whoa!" you shout and they all stop running at once.

With a gentle bump, the sleigh drops to the grass, right next to the presents. Super driving skills – from here, you can easily reach them.

But just as you're gathering them up, a whirring noise comes from the road behind you. You turn to see an electric milk-float heading towards the village green. It must be making deliveries from the dairy so everyone has their milk on Christmas morning.

If you don't get out of here fast, the driver's going to see you.

If you want to hide up the tree, turn to page 64.
To steer the sleigh into Manesh's front garden, turn to page 22.

You'd like to deliver Manesh's present first.

Dasher is thrilled with the idea (Dasher is *always* thrilled with *every* idea) and he leaps into the air, dragging the other reindeer behind him, their legs flailing in all directions as he gallops into the night sky.

He takes you to the countryside, zig-zagging over the meadows like a fairground ride and spinning you around like a sock in a spin-cycle. The view must be lovely from up here, but your eyes are closed and you're clinging to the seat for dear life, and it feels like an age before you reach your destination.

Manesh lives near the village green. When Dasher spots it, he plunges headfirst into the boy's front garden, smashing the picket fence and hammering his head right through the wooden front door.

A baby cries.

An angry face appears in an upstairs window.

"WHAT'S GOING ON OUT THERE?" It's Manesh's mum. She's not happy and she's being really loud about it. "JUSTIN, THERE'S A CHILD IN OUR GARDEN AND A REINDEER'S BUM STICKING OUT OF OUR FRONT DOOR! FETCH A BUCKET OF WATER AND I'LL SOAK THEM FOR WAKING THE BABY UP!"

You've been seen by Manesh's mum and your StoryQuest has come to a very soggy end. Try again and use what you've learnt to complete the challenge.

Go back to the start of the book or turn to page 20 to make a different choice.

You decide to act casual and hope for the best.

You've delivered all three of the presents now, so perhaps it doesn't matter if you're seen by a plane-load of people.

Then again, perhaps it *does*.

As the huge jet reaches your side, you peer in through the windows and come face to face with a long row of passengers.

But they're not the passengers you were expecting.

The whole plane is chock-a-block full of magical characters, some you recognise, some you don't, all smiling widely and waving as they pass. They must be going to Santa's party too! There are elves and pixies, gingerbread people, the Easter Bunny, two small dragons, a coven of good witches, Jack Frost, the tooth fairy and various talking woodland animals wearing clothes.

Santa said you mustn't be seen by another human-being – and you haven't been!

With a sigh of relief, you follow the plane across the frozen landscape to an enormous ice palace. There's a banner above the entrance saying 'WELCOME TO SANTA'S PARTY', and a moat around the outside full of melted chocolate. The walls glisten as if carved out of jewels, the roof shines gold like sunlight and a troop of guards are spinning giant candy-canes in honour of your visit.

And there, in front of the palace, surrounded by a multitude of cheering elves, is Santa himself.

"Welcome," he says, as you land the sleigh. "What a wonderful Stocking Filler you are! You took a few wrong turns along the way, but you kept going and that's what matters. You should be very proud of yourself. Now, before you ring the Magic Yule Bell and start Christmas, do you have the StoryQuest Star for me?"

Yes, I collected the star. Turn to the page number that glittered on the star when you found it.

No, I didn't find the StoryQuest star. Don't worry – turn to page 74.

You point the sleigh into the clouds and fly out of sight from the fishermen.

It's really dark and wet up here though. Even Rudolf's nose isn't lighting the way. And then a deep roll of thunder crashes around you and a flash of lightning zips past the sleigh – you're right in the middle of a terrible storm.

The reindeer are scared. They bolt in different directions and the sleigh tilts. You slide off your seat, somehow managing to stay in the carriage, but watch helplessly as the presents fall over the side and disappear into the ocean.

Oh, dear. You won't be able to deliver them now, but you can always use what you've learnt to try again.

Go back to the start of the book or turn to page 66 to make a different choice.

You swerve right and clip the edge of the tree.

The reindeer keep flying, but the sleigh tilts and somehow you manage to cling to the seat by the tips of your fingers as all three presents go tumbling down to the ground.

Disaster!

As the sleigh levels out, you see the beautifully wrapped gifts there down there on the grass. You'll have to retrieve them, but the village green is quite small and there isn't much room to land without hitting the tree again.

Do you want to risk it?

Yes, I'll land the sleigh. Turn to page 84.

No, I'll jump out and try not to break my legs. Turn to page 82.

# StoryQuest

## CHOOSE THE PAGE - UNLOCK THE ADVENTURE

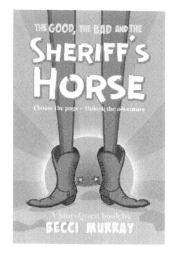

Have you tried these other StoryQuest adventure books? Available now in paperback or eBook.

Laugh along with Billy, as he boosts his brain to the size of Venus in this hilarious five-star chapter book also by Becci Murray.

Or try these very serious poems about really important stuff (like sausages, yaks and toenails) in this illustrated collection of rhyming silliness.

Becci Murray is a British author from Gloucestershire. She used to run a children's entertainment company, where she earned a living playing musical bumps and doing the Hokey Cokey (true story). Her favourite books are by Roald Dahl and she has a life-size BFG sticker on her bedroom wall (well, almost life-size).

You can learn more about Becci or send her a message by visiting the Llama House Children's Books website – she would love to hear from you!

www.llamahousebooks.com

Manufactured by Amazon.ca
Bolton, ON

21505380R00057